Richard Scarry's ABC Word Book

ABRIDGED EDITION

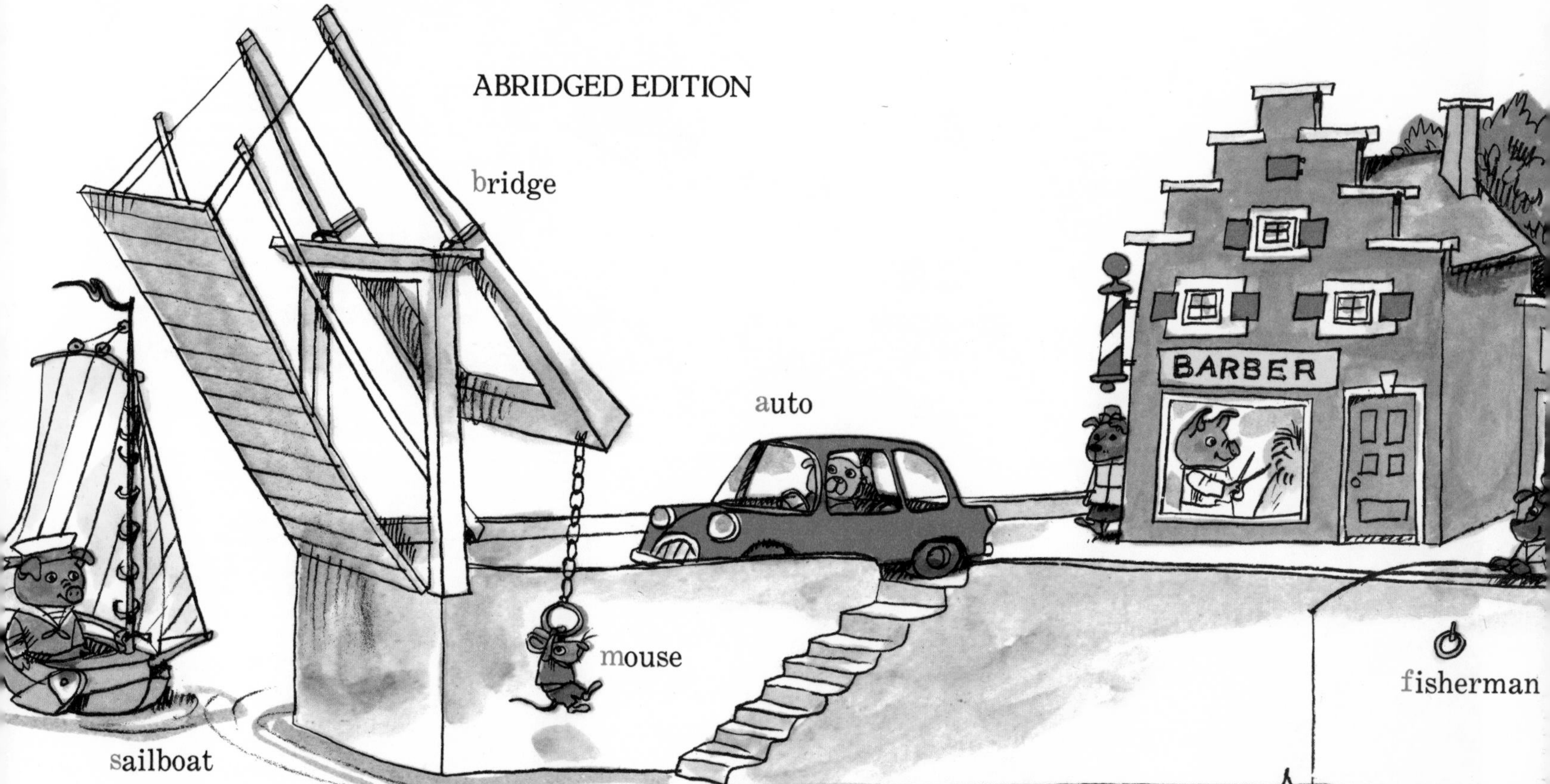

A Random House Book

This title was originally cataloged by the Library of Congress as follows:
Scarry, Richard. ABC word book. New York, Random House [1971] 61 p.
col. illus. 33 cm. SUMMARY: In a brief story for each letter of the alphabet,
the letter is printed in red every time it appears in the text or in the labels for
the many illustrations. [1. Alphabet books] I. Title. PZ7.S327Ab [E]
70–158377 ISBN 0-394-82339-7; 0-394-92339-1 (lib. bdg.)

Published in the United States by Random House, Inc., New York,
and simultaneously in Canada by Random House of Canada Limited, Toronto.
Manufactured in the United States of America.
4567890

Aa

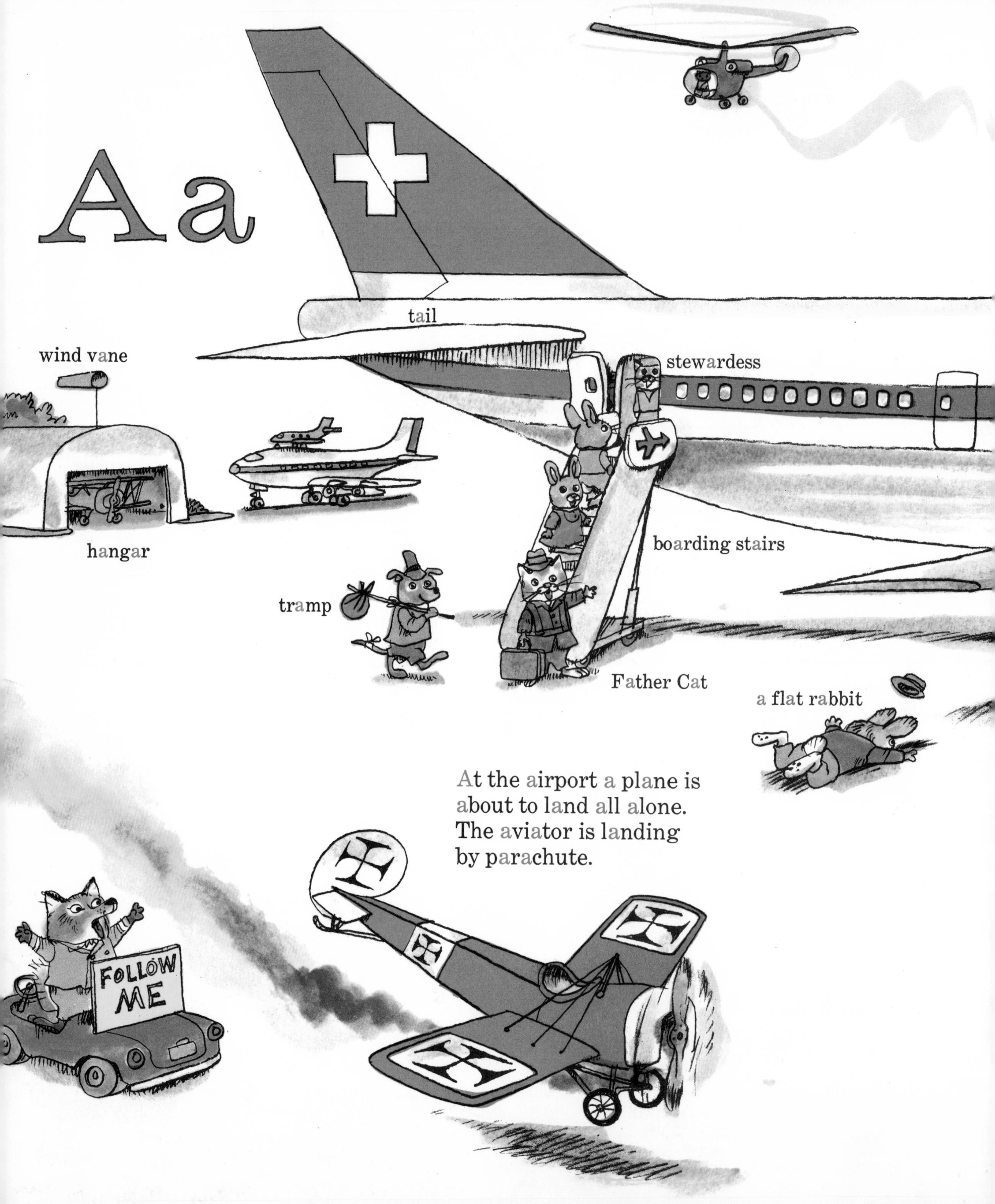

At the airport a plane is
about to land all alone.
The aviator is landing
by parachute.

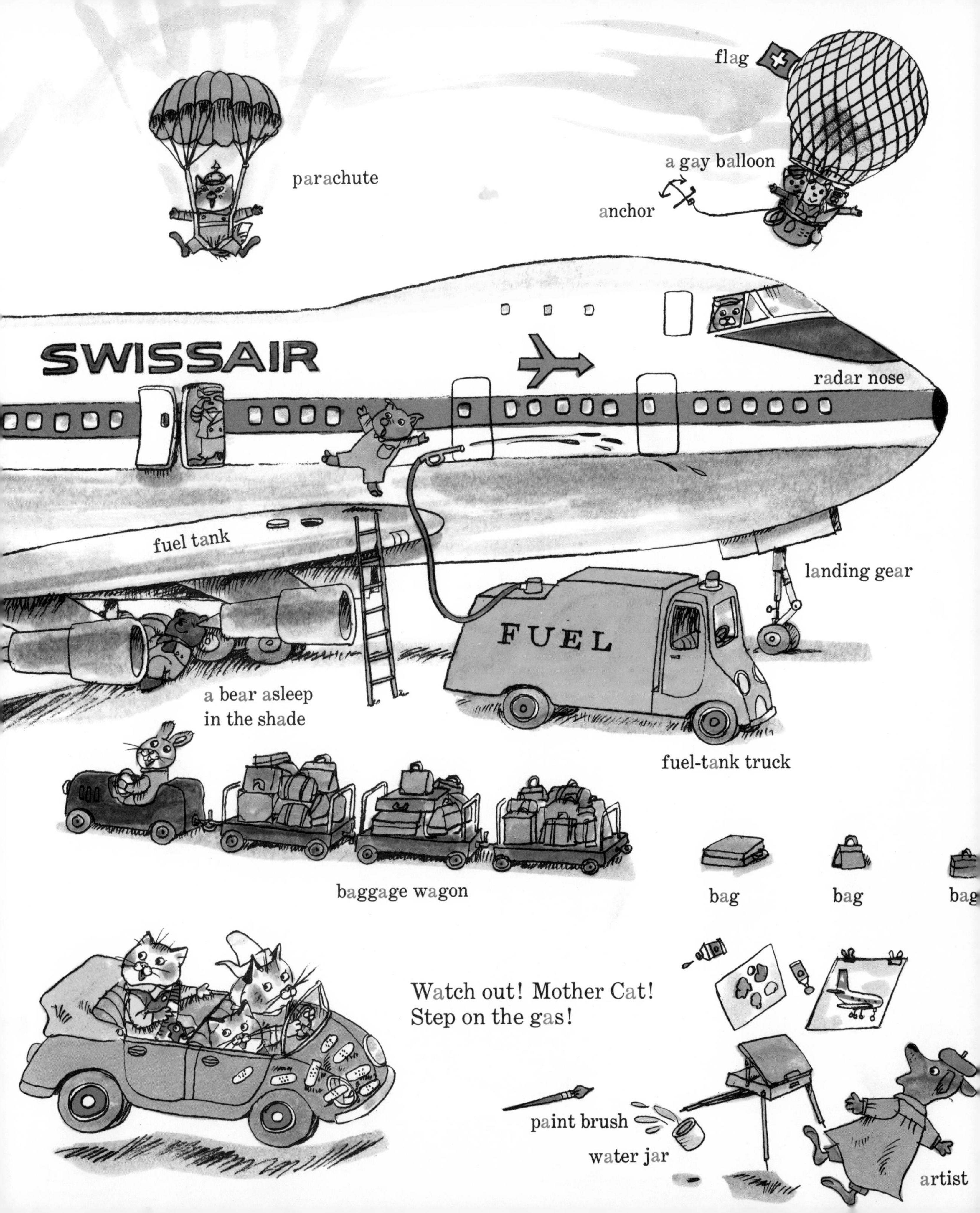

flag
parachute
a gay balloon
anchor
SWISSAIR
radar nose
fuel tank
landing gear
FUEL
a bear asleep
in the shade
fuel-tank truck
baggage wagon
bag
bag
bag
Watch out! Mother Cat!
Step on the gas!
paint brush
water jar
artist

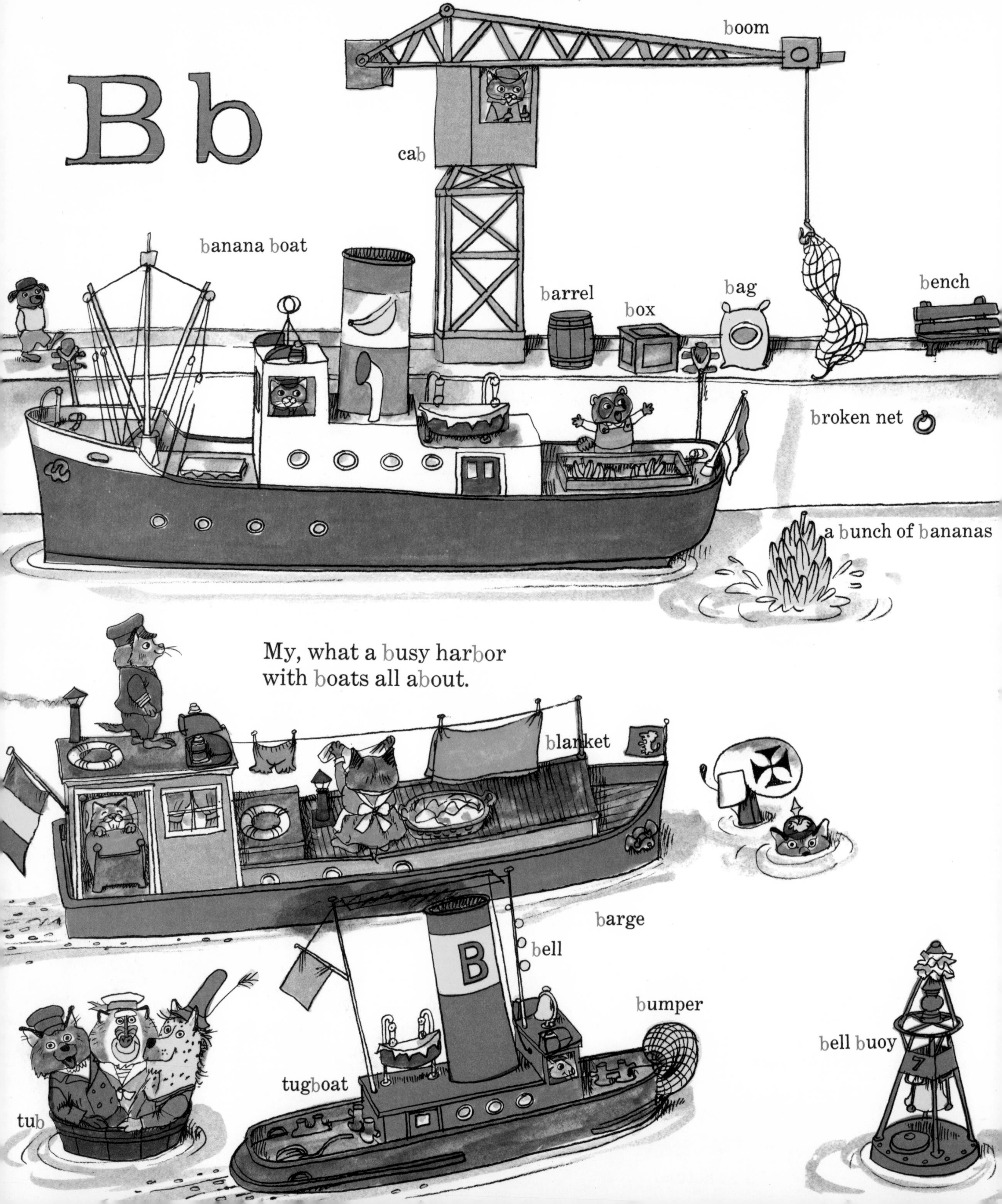
Bb
boom
cab
banana boat
barrel
box
bag
bench
broken net
a bunch of bananas
My, what a busy harbor
with boats all about.
blanket
barge
bell
bumper
bell buoy
tugboat
tub

Captain Salty waves from the bridge of his big, blue ship.

Cc

A crowd came to Tiger Cat's picnic.
Everyone licked ice-cream cones and
danced to the lively music.

A couple of mice served cider
from a cement mixer.

Tiger Cat cooked popcorn.
The cover wasn't closed.
Crackle! Crackle! Pop!
Be careful, Tiger Cat!

Rudolf cracked up.

Crab caught popcorn in his claws.

Lowly danced in a circle with a piece of celery.

Clarence couldn't count the cookies that he ate.

Curly Pig accidentally fell into the center of the cake. CRASH!

What a crazy, cuckoo picnic!

D d

The dizzy, daffy, dopey bulldozer driver! What does he think he is doing? He is dangerous. He has knocked down the drugstore, and the druggist is good and mad.

DETOUR
derrick
board
a dumped-over
dump truck
dirt
rill
a scared ditch-digger
Where is
Huckle
hiding?
ladder
a deep ditch
door
DANGER
a dozen doughnuts
delivery van
DOUGHNUTS

E e

Ernie Elephant and his excellent firemen have just driven up to extinguish an enormous fire. Mother Rabbit is screaming for help. Do not fear! They will save her.

Look at the three firemen on a leaning ladder. Are they going to topple over?

Lowly is sleeping on the stretcher during all the excitement.

Ff

Farmer Fox grows food in his fields for his family. There are five furry foxes hiding in the farmhouse. Can you find them?

flag
farmhouse roof
forest
flower
faucet
fireplace
muffins
flames
flour
floor
one fly
Five flies follow each other in a single file.
a fat fish
Huckle fell flat on his face.
foot
Wolf and his friend Freddy Frog
four fish

G g

What is going on at Greasy George's garage?

Goofy Goose is going to take
a group of gabby goslings to
the picnic grounds. Ugh!
He is groaning at the thought.

a gardener by a glass greenhouse
The telephone is ringing
B-r-r-i-n-g-g-g!
a vegetable garden
Grandma is grinning and giggling.
BARGAIN SALE
glasses
globs of grease
Greasy George is greasing a car with his grease gun. He is wearing gloves.
bang!
clang!
Something is wrong here, but the mechanic is fixing it.
GO
RIGHT
glue
a midget car

H h

Here is a happy home.
However, someone is unhappy.
Father hired a helper to fix
the roof shingles and the helper
hit his thumb with the hammer.
"OUCH!" he howled.

Huckle has
a *very* high hat on
his head and a horn in his hands.
He is blowing hard.

a tree house
branch
shade
Someone is hiding
in a heap of clothes.
hook
hanger
shower
hot water
Hurry, Mother! Something is
happening to the spaghetti.
a hen in
a hurry
honey
pitcher
dish
ketchup
bush
Father is digging a hole
in which to plant a bush
shovel
wheelbarrow

I i

It is a very windy day.
The sails of the windmill were
spinning around fast until Uncle
Irving's kite string tied them up.
The miller is furious. He has
an important order to fill.

Rudolf's diving airplane
lost its wings in flight.
Rudolf is going swimming
with his friends.

Willy, a little imp,
is licking an ice-cream
cone and spilling it on
Uncle Irving's shirt.

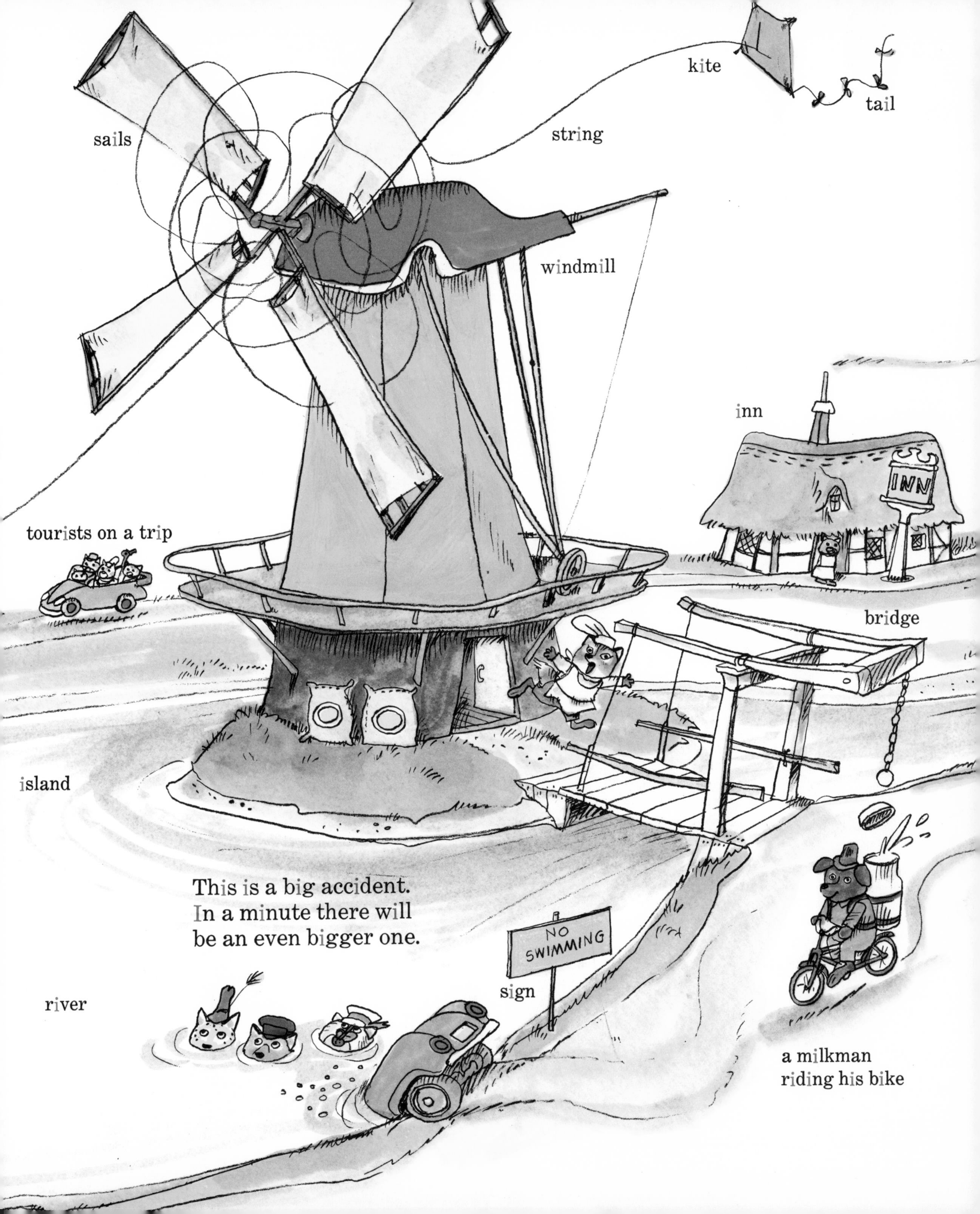

This is a big accident.
In a minute there will
be an even bigger one.

J j

Hilda just jammed a grapefruit
between her jaws and went *c-r-u-n-c-h*.
Was it juicy, Hilda?

a jet pilot on a joy-ride

parachute jumper

Janitor Joe enjoys
driving his jeep.

This juggler
is juggling
jars of jelly.

jacket

jug

jack-o'-lantern

K k

The king is having a snack.
He is licking a pickle.
Kangaroo is skating in with
a cake she has baked for the king.
Would you like to share his snack?

ketchup
kettle
stick
cook book
cook
a thick steak
a leaky bucket
kangaroo
a kiss
smack!
Huckle has a pumpkin in the back of his truck.
skate
pumpkin
truck

L l

A large steamroller is rolling wildly over the land. Look out, all you people, or you will be flattened!

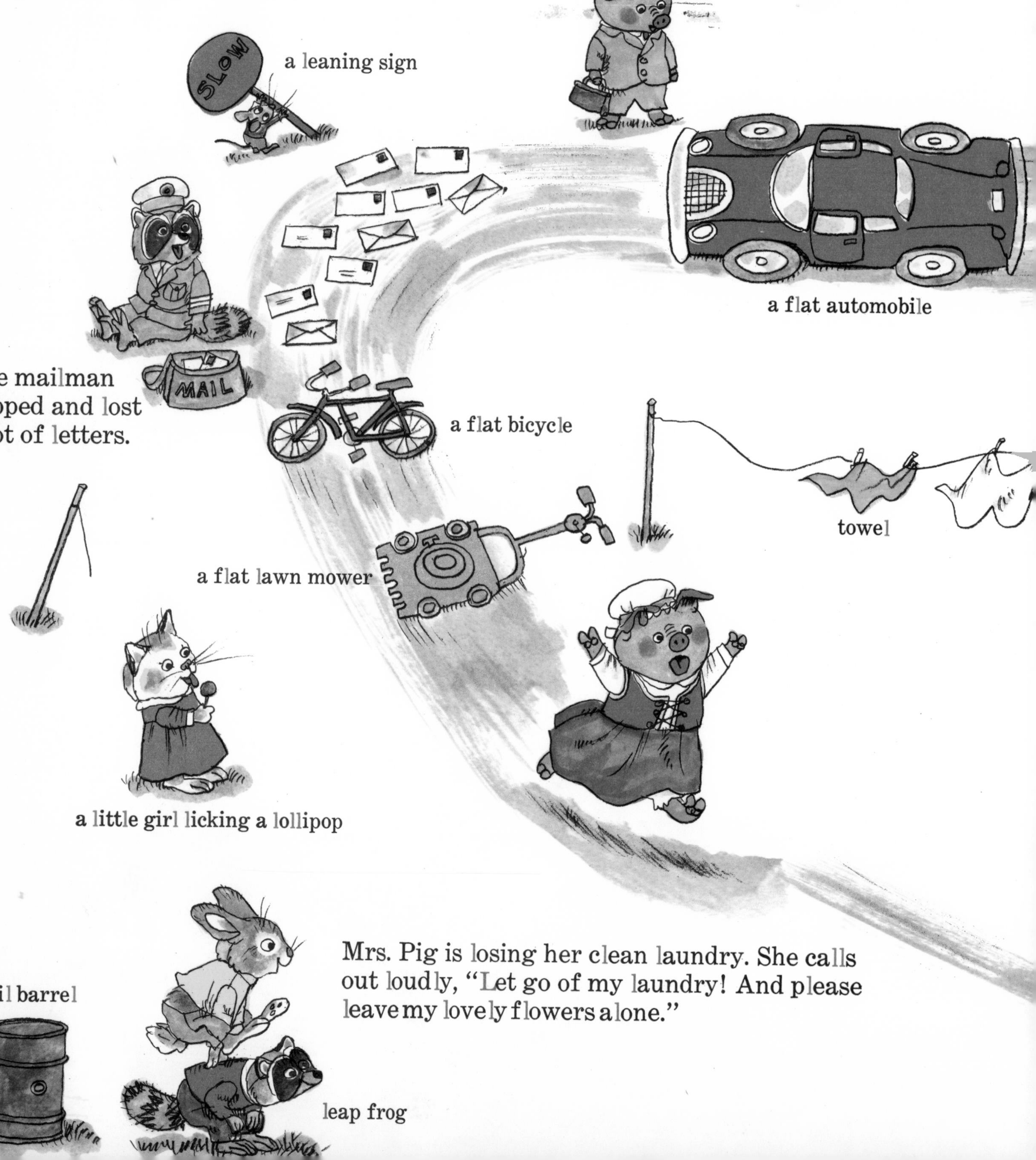

The mailman slipped and lost a lot of letters.

Mrs. Pig is losing her clean laundry. She calls out loudly, "Let go of my laundry! And please leave my lovely flowers alone."

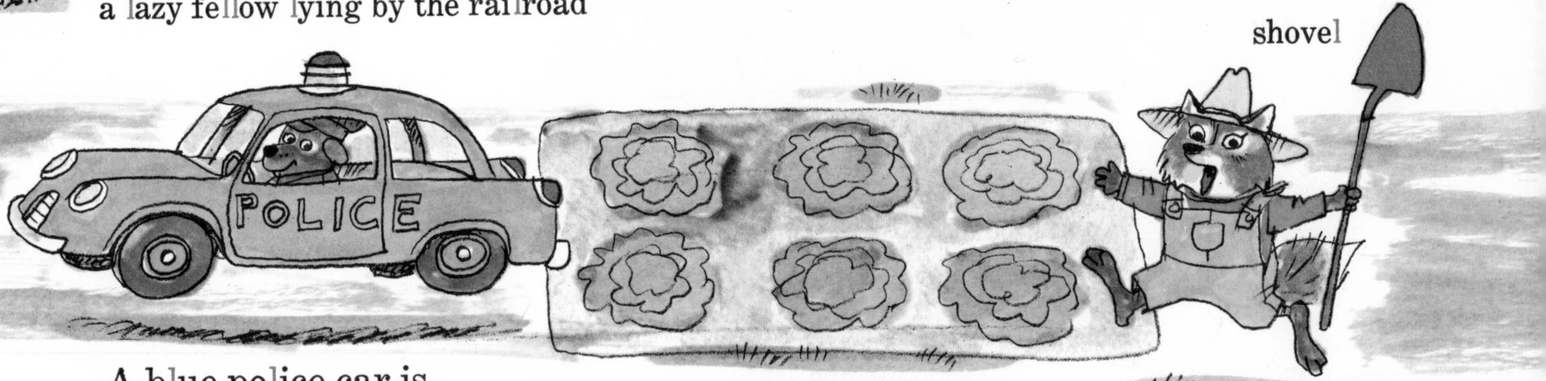

a load of long logs
a lazy fellow lying by the railroad
locomotive
shovel
A blue police car is
following the silly gorilla
in the steamroller.
POLICE
a field of flat lettuce
clothes line
Huckle and Lowly!
What are you doing
with that loony gorilla?
a tall lily plan
a yellow steamroller

Mm

drum
mouse
midget car
merry firemen making music
cement mixer
ambulance
medicine
instruments
ice-cream man
ICE CREAM
M.D.
bump!
Doctor Monday on a bumpy road

Something is the matter
with Mommy's motor.
A mechanic is trying
to make it go.
Father Pig is stuck
in the messy, muddy road.
Is he ever mad! Oh, my!

Nn
airplane
orange crane
nose
Rudolf's plane landed in a pond.
A crane yanked it out.
a broken fence
net
a bunch of bananas
NORTH MAIN
sign
a policeman running
another runner
in pink pants
a nice nursemaid
and an infant napping

Another airplane landed in the pond—and then another.
No more, please. That is certainly enough!

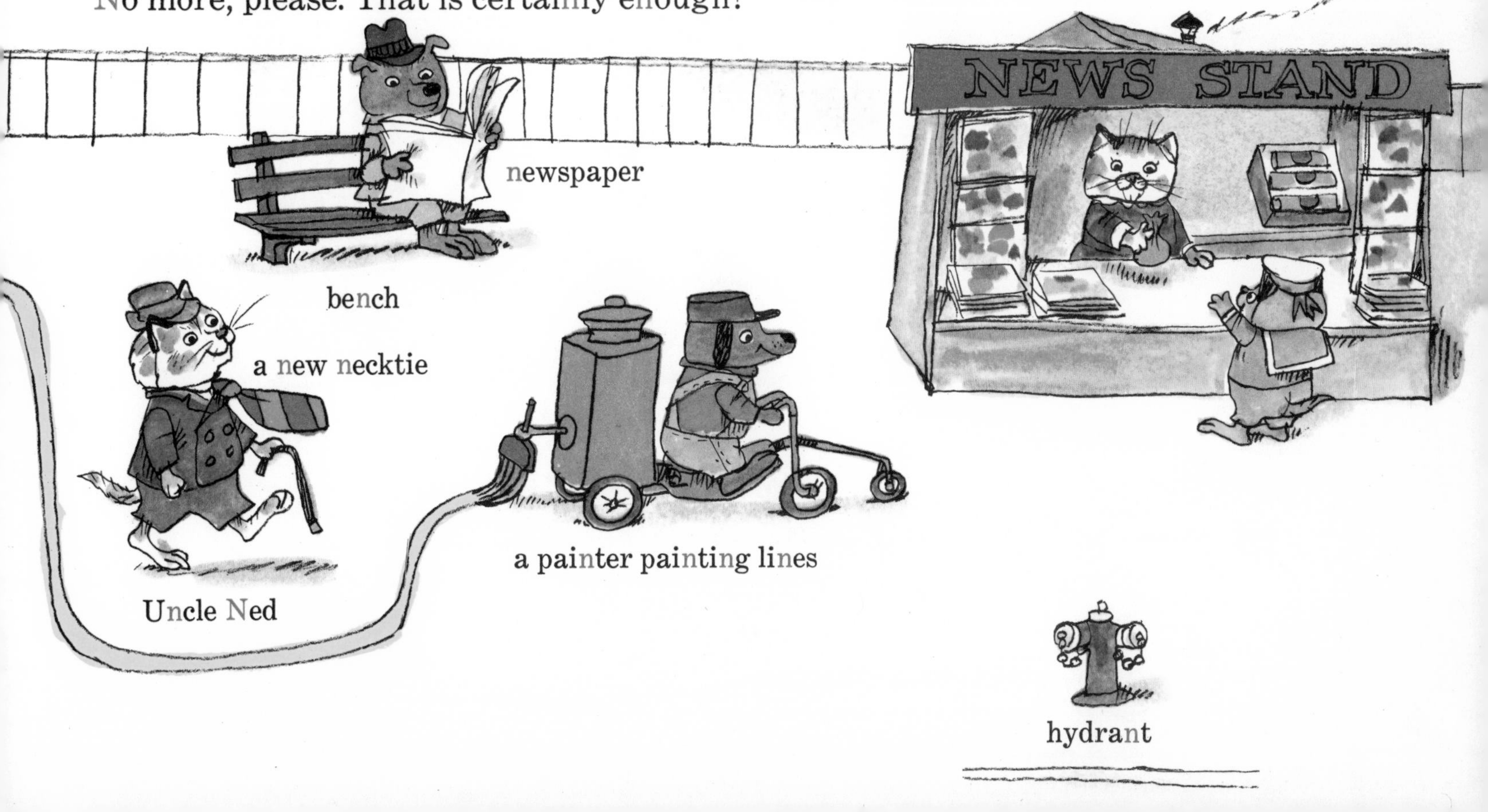

Oo

Oh, my! See how many people have come down to the harbor to see the boats dock.

Someone forgot to stop.
The boat is going down
to the bottom of the harbor.

P p

Pretty Polly Pig is having a party.
She is playing the piano. *Plink! Plink!*
All the people are happy.

Q q

mosquito

The Queen is playing croquet with her friends.
They seem to be quarreling. Please! Let's be quiet!

Quite a nice shot, Queenie!

The queen in her quilted robe

Rr

The Rapid Rabbits were racing the River Rascals in a rowboat race up the river. The steerer steered right onto a rock. *C-r-u-n-c-h!* The race was over. He was in a furious rage.

Rhinoceros is rather peculiar. He prefers not to get wet when he goes into the water.

A waiter is carrying a tray of fruit to a customer. Who left that chair where someone would surely trip over it?

Ss

Daddy Pig came into the house and kissed Mommy.
"What's for supper?" he asked.
"Your seven silly cousins are visiting us for several days," answered Mommy. "They wish to cook and serve our meals to us. They are making a super surprise supper now."
"It surely does smell delicious," said Daddy. "Let's see what it is that smells so good."
Oh! Such a sight they saw!

Sam was washing dishes in the sink.

Silas was searching for some stockings in the storage barrel.

Sandy was adding soap and sticky syrup to the stew.

Sidney was slowly stirring the stew.

Stanley was spilling a strainer of slippery spaghetti.

Simon was pouring sweet strawberries into the simmering soup.

T t

Take a look at the terrible accident.
A train has hit a trailer truck that
contained ten thousand tomatoes.
What a sight!

Uu

Duck is busy unloading nuts out of his dump truck.

Sergeant Murphy is shouting loudly, "Don't clutter up the avenue!"

V v

A flivver is driving through a village and over a very high viaduct. This roving family is going to visit relatives.

W w

a whirring,
twirling windmill

two wiggling
wrestlers

Owl growing wheat
in a meadow

a girl watching
at the window

wrench

Lowly Worm
inside a watermelon

two fowl squawking

a walnut on a wall

X x

A fox and an ox are mixing
alphabet soup in a box.
It is excellent exercise.

Y y

Yak is playing
with his Yo-Yo.

Why is the roly-poly pig
crying? He has his own toy.

Z z
a hat that is
the wrong size
blazer
a zebra in
a zipper jacket
chimpanzee
Lowly is snoozing.
exit
nix
razzle dazzle
yoo hoo
tin lizzie
a dozing baby
buzzer
Yellow stripes show
the safety zone.
Izzy Lizard is dizzy. He is walking zigzag.

Aa Bb Cc

Gg Hh Ii

Mm Nn Oo

Ss Tt Uu

Xx Yy